1, 2, 3 y los colores de querido dragón

Dear Dragon's Colors 1, 2, 3

por/by Margaret Hillert
ilustrado por/Illustrated by David Schimmell

NORWOOD HOUSE PRESS

Queridos padres y maestros:

La serie para lectores principiantes es una colección de lecturas cuidadosamente escritas, muchas de las cuales ustedes recordarán de su propia infancia. Cada libro comprende palabras de uso frecuente en español e inglés y, a través de la repetición, le ofrece al niño la oportunidad de practicarlas. Los detalles adicionales de las ilustraciones refuerzan la historia y le brindan la oportunidad de ayudar a su niño a desarrollar el lenguaje oral y la comprensión.

Primero, léale el cuento al niño; después deje que él lea las palabras con las que está familiarizado y pronto, podrá leer solito todo el cuento. En cada paso, elogie el esfuerzo del niño para que se sienta más confiado como lector independiente. Hable sobre las ilustraciones y anime al niño a relacionar el cuento con su propia vida.

Sobre todo, la parte más importante de la experiencia de la lectura es ¡divertirse y disfrutarla!

Shannon Cannon

Shannon Cannon
Consultora de lectoescritura

Dear Caregiver,

The *Beginning-to-Read* series is a carefully written collection of readers, many of which you may remember from your own childhood. This book, *Dear Dragon's Day with Father*, was written over 30 years after the first *Dear Dragon* books were published. The *New Dear Dragon* series features the same elements of the earlier books, such as text comprised of common sight words. These sight words provide your child with ample practice reading the words that appear most frequently in written text. The many additional details in the pictures enhance the story and offer the opportunity for you to help your child expand oral language skills and develop comprehension.

Begin by reading the story to your child, followed by letting him or her read familiar words and soon your child will be able to read the story independently. At each step of the way, be sure to praise your reader's efforts to build his or her confidence as an independent reader. Discuss the pictures and encourage your child to make connections between the story and his or her own life.

Above all, the most important part of the reading experience is to have fun and enjoy it!

Shannon Cannon,
Literacy Consultant

Norwood House Press • P.O. Box 316598 • Chicago, Illinois 60631
For more information about Norwood House Press please visit our website at *www.norwoodhousepress.com* or call 866-565-2900.

Text copyright ©2012 by Margaret Hillert. Illustrations and cover design copyright ©2012 by Norwood House Press, Inc. All rights reserved. No part of this book may be reproduced or utilized in any form or by any means without written permission from the publisher.

LIBRARY OF CONGRESS CATALOGING-IN-PUBLICATION DATA

Hillert, Margaret.
  [Dear dragon's colors 1, 2, 3. Spanish & English]
  1, 2, 3 y los colores de querido dragón = Dear dragon's colors 1, 2, 3 / por/by Margaret Hillert ; ilustrado por/illustrated by David Schimmell ; [translated by Eida del Risco].
    p. cm. -- (A beginning-to-read book)
  Includes word list.
  Summary: "A boy and his pet dragon have fun learning about counting and colors. Carefully translated to include English and Spanish text "--Provided by publisher.
  ISBN-13: 978-1-59953-470-1 (library edition : alk. paper)
  ISBN-10: 1-59953-470-3 (library edition : alk. paper)
  [1. Dragons--Fiction. 2. Color--Fiction. 3. Counting. 4. Spanish language books--Bilingual.] I. Schimmell, David ; ill. II. Del Risco, Eida. III. Title. IV. Title: Dear dragon's colors 1, 2, 3. V. Title: Uno, dos, tres y los colores de querido dragon. VI. Title: Dear dragon's colors one, two, three.
  PZ73.H5572005 2011
  [E]--dc23

                                    2011016651

Manufactured in the United States of America in North Mankato, Minnesota.
178N—072011

Juega conmigo.
Ven a jugar conmigo.
Me gusta jugar
con carros.

Play with me.
Come play with me.
I like to play with cars.

3

1 carrito **rojo**.
Puede correr y correr.
Es divertido jugar
con un carrito **rojo**.

1 little **red** car.
It can go, go, go.
It is fun to play with
a little **red** car.

1 carrito **rojo**.

1 little **red** car.

Yo tengo **2** carritos **azules**.
Puedo hacer que suban y bajen.

I have **2** little **blue** cars.
I can make them go up and down.

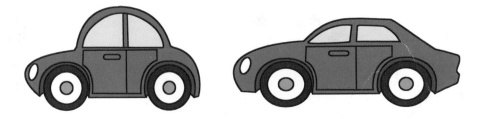

2 carritos **azules**.

2 little **blue** cars.

Tengo **3** carritos **amarillos**.
Los carros **amarillos** son bonitos.
Pueden entrar y salir.

I have **3** little **yellow** cars.
Yellow cars are pretty.
They can go in and out.

3 carritos **amarillos**.

3 little **yellow** cars.

Tengo **4** carritos **verdes**.
El **verde** es bueno.
Me gusta el **verde**.

I have **4** little **green** cars.
Green is good.
I like **green**.

4 carritos **verdes**.

4 little **green** cars.

Tengo **5** carritos **anaranjados**.

Ay, ay, ay.

¿Qué es esto?

Esto no es bueno.

I have **5** little **orange** cars.

Oh, oh, oh.

What is this?

This is not good.

5 carritos **anaranjados**.

5 little **orange** cars.

Tengo **6** carritos **marrones**.
Corran, carros, corran.
Esto es muy, muy divertido.

I have **6** little **brown** cars.
Go, cars. Go.
This is fun, fun, fun.

6 carritos **marrones**.

6 little **brown** cars.

Tengo **7** carritos **morados**.
A mamá le gusta el **morado**.
A mí también me gusta el **morado**.

I have **7** little **purple** cars.
Mother likes **purple**.
I like **purple**, too.

7 carritos **morados**.

7 little **purple** cars.

Tengo **8** carritos **rosados**.
Qué bonitos.
Rosados, **rosados**, **rosados**.

I have **8** little **pink** cars.
How pretty.
Pink, **pink**, **pink**.

8 carritos **rosados**.

8 little **pink** cars.

Tengo **9** carritos **negros**.
Esto es bueno.

I have **9** little **black** cars.
This is good.

9 carritos **negros**.

9 little **black** cars.

Tengo **10** carritos **blancos**.
Podemos divertirnos con los carros.

I have **10** little **white** cars.
We can have fun with the cars.

10 carritos **blancos**.

10 little **white** cars.

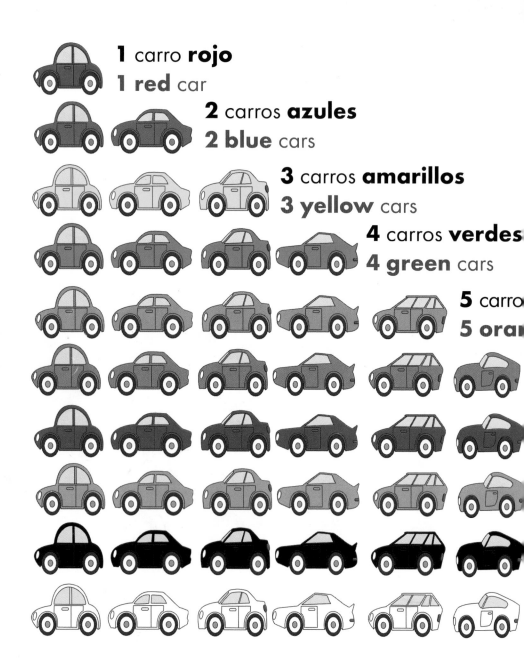

1 carro **rojo**
1 red car

2 carros **azules**
2 blue cars

3 carros **amarillos**
3 yellow cars

4 carros **verdes**
4 green cars

5 carros
5 oran

anaranjados

ge cars

5 carros marrones

5 brown cars

 7 carros morados

7 purple cars

 8 carros rosados

8 pink cars

 9 carros negros

9 black cars

 **10 carros blancos**

10 white cars.

¡Caramba!
Mira esto.
Tantos carros.
Tantos, tantos carros.

Wow!
Look at this.
So many cars.
So many, many cars.

Tú estás conmigo
y yo estoy contigo.
Qué divertido.
Qué divertido, querido dragón.

Here you are with me.
And here I am with you.
What fun.
What fun, dear dragon.

READING REINFORCEMENT

The following activities support the findings of the National Reading Panel that determined the most effective components for reading instruction are: Phonemic Awareness, Phonics, Vocabulary, Fluency, and Text Comprehension.

Phonemic Awareness: The /ar/ sound

Sound Substitution: Say each of the following words to your child and ask your child to tell you which two words rhyme:

park, dark, pack	jar, jam, far	yam, yarn, barn
shark, shack, bark	cage, barge, large	harp, tap, tarp
part, mart, mat	had, card, hard	

Phonics: /ar/ Phonograms

1. Explain to your child that sometimes, the letter **r** after a vowel changes the sound of the vowel (for example, can/car).

2. Fold a piece of paper in half the long way twice.

3. Draw a line down the folds to divide the paper into four parts.

4. Write the phonograms **-ar**, **-ard**, **-arm**, and **-art** in separate columns at the top of the page.

5. Write the following words on separate (small) pieces of paper or index cards:

car	cart	card	farm	far
part	dart	star	tart	yard
harm	smart	lard	arm	tar
charm	jar	hard	chart	bar

6. Have your child underline the phonogram in each word.

Vocabulary: Color Words

1. Write the following words on separate pieces of paper or index cards:

black	blue	brown	green	orange
pink	purple	red	white	yellow

2. Read each word to your child and ask your child to repeat it.

3. Ask your child to trace over the letters with crayon or marker, using the corresponding color (you might suggest that your child revisit the book for help).

4. Mix the words up. Point to a word and ask your child to read it. Provide clues if your child needs them. For example:

This is the color of pumpkins. (orange)

Grass is this color in spring. (green)

Panda bears and zebras are these two colors. (black and white)

Fluency: Echo Reading

1. Reread the story to your child at least two more times while your child tracks the print by running a finger under the words as they are read. Ask your child to read the words he or she knows with you.

2. Reread the story, stopping after each sentence or page to allow your child to read (echo) what you have read. Repeat echo reading and let your child take the lead.

Text Comprehension: Discussion Time

1. Ask your child to retell the sequence of events in the story.

2. To check comprehension, ask your child the following questions:

- How many pink cars does the boy have?
- What happened to the orange cars?
- What color do the boy and his mother both like?
- What is your favorite color? Why?